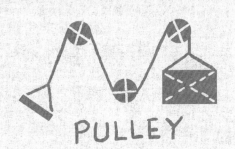

PULLEY

LEVER

AXLE

SCREW

WHEEL

AXLE

INCLINED PLANE

WEDGE

SCREW

SCREW

PULLEY

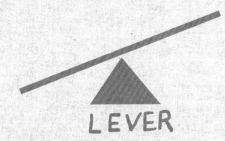

LEVER

WEDGE

INCLINED PLANE

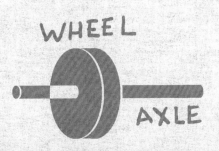

WHEEL

AXLE

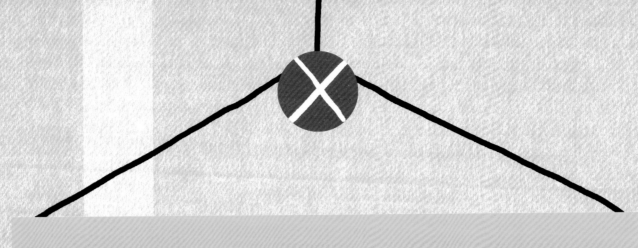

LIFT, MIX, FLING!
Machines Can Do Anything

BY Lola M. Schaefer

ILLUSTRATED BY James Yang

Greenwillow Books
An Imprint of HarperCollinsPublishers

For Adam
—L. M. S.

For my science teachers.
It was always my favorite class of the day.
—J. Y.

Lift, Mix, Fling! Machines Can Do Anything
Text copyright © 2022 by Lola M. Schaefer
Illustrations copyright © 2022 by James Yang
All rights reserved. Manufactured in Italy.
For information address HarperCollins Children's Books,
a division of HarperCollins Publishers,
195 Broadway, New York, NY 10007.
www.harpercollinschildrens.com

The illustrations were created digitally in Photoshop.
The text type is 20-point Gotham Book.

Library of Congress Cataloging-in-Publication Data is available.

ISBN 9780062457103 (hardcover)

22 23 24 25 26 RTLO 10 9 8 7 6 5 4 3 2 1
First Edition

GREENWILLOW BOOKS

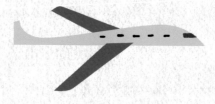

Machines use force
to make work easier.
They help us . . .

climb a tall tree,
or sail the lake,
explore the planets,
or make a shake.

Simple machines have
one or two parts,

like a spoon, a knife,
the wheels on carts.

A lens that turns
for close-up views,

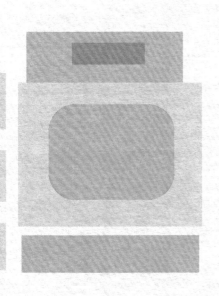

and lids on jars
are types of screws.

An inclined plane
helps push or roll.

These wheels and axles
go for a stroll.

One simple machine
uses an edge

to open and pry.

That's the wedge.

These levers move loads
with a bit of might.
And pulleys lift weight
clear out of sight.

Think of a shovel,
staircases, too,

a fan,

a skate,

the ramps at the zoo.

But some machines
do more than one thing.
They hover and soar,

spring and fling.

Compound machines
are two or more
simple machines working
together. They help us . . .

launch a rocket up and away,

or cut and bale
late-summer hay.

Tractors can plow,
grade, or carry.

Trucks mix and pour.

Ships hold and ferry.

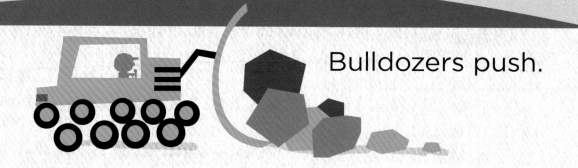

Bulldozers push.

Chainsaws cut poles.

Sprinklers spray plants,

and augers dig holes.

Drills buzz and whirr,

and jackhammers crack.

Clocks beep and clang,

Dryers fluff clothes.

Locks secure doors.

Toasters warm bread,

and vacuums clean floors.

No matter the work,
big or small,
a machine can help
do it all!

A MACHINE is a tool that does work.

WORK is the transfer of energy from one object to another.

ENERGY is a measure of how much work something can do. Machines need a source of energy, such as a twist or shove from your hand or arm.

A machine reduces the amount of **FORCE** (a push or pull) needed to move an object.

SIMPLE MACHINES have few or no moving parts. The six simple machines are: wheel and axle, pulley, wedge, lever, screw, inclined plane.

A COMPOUND MACHINE is two or more simple machines that work together. Some compound machines, like a roller coaster or a robot, are made up of hundreds of simple machines.

Look around your home and find the simple and compound machines that you use every day.